Death Row Follies

and Other Stories

Death Row Follies

and Other Stories

by Jack Albert

Lofty Publishing
Rockville, Maryland

The stories contained in this book have previously been published as follows:

"Byron": in the hardcover anthology *Cat Crimes Through Time* edited by Ed Gorman and published by Carroll and Graf,

"The Cheat": in *Lucid Moon,*

"The Inquisition": in *The Ultimate Writer,*

"Death Row Follies": in *Crystal Drum* and

"The Long Wait": in *The Veneration Quarterly.*

Cover background credit: ©iStockphoto.com/Sasha Martynchuk

ISBN 978-0-9843824-0-8 (paperback)
ISBN 978-0-9843824-1-5 (e-book)

To My Mother Anna

And the Memory of My Father Otto Leopold

Contents

Byron

Lynn chose the long way, crossing over to the
other side of Beirut with her friend, Byron the
cat. They left the Christian side and went by
taxi to Damascus, some ninety kilometers away.
There, she found another cab with an Armenian
driver who was returning to the Moslem side.
Armenians were considered neutral in the con-
flict, and allowed to operate in both zones. She
gave him no hint that she understood Arabic.

Her orders were simple. The Commander
had given her the key to an apartment and an
address. The information came from Mossad's
resident in Ras-Beirut, who was recently trans-
ferred. He owed the Commander a favor. The
rest was up to her.

She looked at herself in her hand mirror. Her
hair was combed and rolled up in a bun. The

gray had appeared soon after she'd stopped using the dye. There were also wrinkles around her eyes. She wondered whether Boulos would still find her attractive. She had taken the assignment in order to find him. Yet, she had no idea where to look for him or whether he was still alive.

At seven in the morning, the taxi reached Ras-Beirut, and stopped in front of a two story building with arcades and columns, and a roof covered with red bricks. Each floor had a balcony looking out on the street.

She stepped out of the Mercedes, her left arm wrapped around Byron, waiting for the driver to unload her two suitcases from the trunk. A man with a white armband came running out of the building, revolver in hand. In broken Arabic, the cabby explained that he had driven the English lady all the way from Damascus.

"I am Aziz, of Security," the man in the white armband said. "Open the luggage."

In the soft nylon suitcase there were dresses and toiletries. The other suitcase had a hard shell and contained shoes and undergarments. Aziz felt with his hand around the bottom of the first suitcase and nodded his head. He examined the bottom of the second suitcase and raised his eyebrows. He pulled a switchblade from his breast pocket when a jeep approached at high speed, tooting its horn. The teenage driver kept looking in the rear-view mirror. In the back, a man toyed with an AK-47 submachine gun, aiming it all around, probably trying to impress the local females.

Aziz cursed, and disappeared around the corner. A little later, he came back at the wheel of a noisy half-track, and went chasing the jeep.

The cabby moved the two pieces of luggage inside the apartment. He wrote something on a piece of paper.

"If you need a taxi again, here is my telephone number. My name is Vartkes."

She put on the tea-pot to boil and stepped out on the balcony. A young woman came down the outside stairs, leading a boy by the hand. The boy carried a tin box. A car stopped in front of the building. A uniformed man jumped out and saluted the woman. She and the boy disappeared down the street.

Suddenly, Lynn heard two bangs coming from the back of the apartment. Seconds later, there was another bang. The apartment consisted of a large living-room, a den, a kitchen and a bedroom in the rear. She placed her ear against the back wall of the bedroom and listened. There were no more bangs.

She locked the apartment door, leaving Byron to keep an eye on things. Along the street, the walls were covered with proclamations and hand-painted portraits of Nasser. Four blocks away, she found a cinder-block structure with a sign that read: "Andeel's Supermarket." A young man in an Orioles cap stood at the door, inviting people in.

The store was filled with noisy locals, nervously shopping by candlelight. She was told that the generator was out of gasoline. The smell of rotting fish turned her stomach. She purchased a bottle of Evian water, a few cans of tuna for herself and Byron, and a copy of *The Daily Star*.

"Excuse me, madam," someone said in decent English. "Can I help carry the groceries?"

It was the young man in the Orioles cap.

She smiled and told him she could manage by herself, but he insisted. He said that his name was Usamah, and that he was a freshman at the American University. Since the university was temporarily closed, he was working at Andeel's. On the way, he asked why she was in Beirut. She told him that she was covering the war for *The Times* of London.

When they reached the apartment, she tipped him with a Lebanese five-pound note. He thanked her and told her he could be reached at the store, "should you need anything."

Byron waited at the door, mewing for food. After devouring a can of tuna, he went to sleep on the balcony.

She joined him outside to read the paper. She gazed at the headline: "Presidential Palace Attacked. President Chamoun Safe." She thought about her mission, which was to kill Rustom, the head of a Moslem militia group. She wondered about the mysterious noises she'd heard.

"Come, Byron," she said. "We're going for a little walk."

In order to reach the back of the building, she had to cross a natural barrier of overgrown grasses threaded with morning glory that surrounded a clearing. There was one big wall, and a low window, closed off with cement. There was also a rusty door guarded by a youth in blue jeans. He sat on a chair, snoring, his face hidden under a newspaper. The butt of a pistol stuck out of his back pocket. Her heart sounded in her ears.

Perhaps Boulos was behind that door. She could shout his name, but didn't because of the guard. She went back to her apartment and once more listened at the back wall. There were no noises.

That night, the sound of artillery woke her. The shelling seemed to be coming from the Christian side. It was answered with a barrage of rockets. This sound she'd heard before.

After the next salvo, the building lost its electric power. She heard steps outside her door, one discrete tap then another. Carefully, she opened it. The beam of her flashlight caught the distorted features of Usamah, the young man from the store. He whispered that he had information that could make both of them a lot of money. He knew where a kidnapped man was being held and was prepared to show her.

Something did not sound right. She told him that she needed time to contact the home office.

"You must come right now," he said. "This prisoner is constantly being moved."

She told him she was going to call her boss, and began to close the door. Usamah shoved his foot in the way, pulled out a gun and placed it against her temple.

"Come with me. Quickly."

A cold sweat trickled down her spine as she thought of her husband, Boulos. Six months before, while on a night mission with eight of his men, he had been ambushed. The next day, they'd found eight mutilated bodies, but no trace of Boulos. Later, there had been rumors that he was held hostage. She started to shiver. Horrible scenes she had read about came back to her, but this time, it was her own dead body she saw dumped with tens of others on the banks of Nahr Ibrahim.

Usamah made her walk three short blocks to an apartment building. The entrance was narrow. He released his grip and pushed her in. She heard the sound of a rat scurrying past, followed by a familiar meow. Usamah followed her in.

From above, Byron suddenly landed on Usamah's head, puffing and clawing. The man tried to fight, but the cat snarled and refused to let go. She kicked Usamah in the groin, and the gun fell on the floor. She picked it up and pointed it at him.

She tied his shirt around his mouth and took him to the rear of the apartment building. She opened a door, walked down a few steps and reached the bottom of the elevator shaft. Using his belt, she fastened his hands to a metal pipe. It would be a while before anyone found him.

As she got near her apartment, she slowed her pace. Byron, who had been following her, slowed down.

"Thanks," she said to the cat.

The next morning, she woke up at seven. Somewhere, a loudspeaker was broadcasting taped chants of the Moslem morning prayer. The woman from upstairs came with her son.

"I am Madame Rustom and this is my son Antar," she said proudly.

"What a darling boy," Lynn said, playing with his shiny black hair.

The boy opened the tin box and offered her an expended machine gun shell.

"Thank you," Lynn said.

Inside the box were four more spent bullets and two large artillery shell fragments.

"He collects them," Madame said, "and exchanges them with his friends. Antar, stop bothering the lady and leave us alone for a few minutes."

Rustom was here, Lynn thought, the man the Commander wanted dead. Should she complete her mission or disobey the Commander's orders and keep looking for her husband?

Meanwhile, Madame noticed a brass amulet on the wall. It was in the shape of a cat's eye.

"What a nice souvenir."

"It's from Damascus," Lynn said, back in the conversation.

"Do you know the origin of this kind of amulet?"

"No."

"In ancient times, Arab warriors used to wear them into battle, believing they provided protection from harm."

Lynn smiled.

Madame expressed her admiration for the style of Lynn's clothes. She tried to find out which part of England she was from, if it rained there, and why she had come to Lebanon. Lynn told her she was a reporter.

"Very important work," Madame said, showing a beautiful set of teeth. "Come, Antar. We must go."

The boy closed the tin box, in spite of Byron's curiosity for its contents.

Madame shook Lynn's hand, and wished her a pleasant stay.

Lynn waited for them to depart, and made a telephone call to Vartkes.

Next, she had a cup of tea outside. A man in his mid-thirties stood on the upstairs balcony, and waved in the direction of Madame and her son.

Lynn recalled the information of the Mossad agent. Boulos and his men had been ambushed by Rustom. That man probably still held her husband.

Madame and her son disappeared around the corner. Byron became agitated, and went looking for the tin box.

"Come back, Byron," Lynn said. "Back here, Byron."

Interested, Rustom craned his neck over the ledge.

"Miss," he said, "why do you bother with this useless cat? Many of us are so poor we can't feed our children, while you foreigners have money to throw away on pets."

He pulled out a machine gun and sprayed a hail of bullets in the direction where Byron had disappeared.

"You bloody bastard," she said, her hands on her ears.

"Anyone who starves our people will be treated this way," he said, putting a new clip in his weapon.

She uselessly looked for something to throw.

He laughed and went back into his apartment.

She returned to the rear of the building, and hid in the grass. The youth in jeans was taking a stroll. She threw a pebble a small distance away. The young man pulled out his gun and came to investigate. As he passed in front of her, she stuck out her foot and tripped him. He hit the ground head first, losing the gun. He lay there, moaning softly. She knocked him unconscious with the gun, and used his handkerchief to tie his hands behind his back.

In his pocket she found a key. It opened the rusty door. The only furniture inside the filthy room was a bare metal bed. The smell of urine assaulted her. After she got used to the dark, she saw a thin man lying on the bed. He had a long black beard.

"Boulos?" she said.

There was no answer.

"I am Lynn, your wife."

She came closer and touched his face. She felt his warm tears on her fingers. Slowly, she took him into her arms and helped him stand up. He took a couple of slow steps toward the door. She ordered the whimpering youth to come in, tied him to a post, and filled his mouth with a piece of towel.

"We'll stop here for a moment," she said, opening her apartment door. "To see if Byron is back."

Aziz yanked her gun away, and pulled her inside.

"We were sitting here, waiting for you," Rustom said.

He pointed to Boulos.

"You know him?"

Slowly, she pushed Boulos near where Rustom was standing. She was only a few feet from Aziz.

Rustom asked Aziz for her gun, and pointed to something on the balcony.

"I don't like cats," he said. "Didn't I tell you to get rid of it?"

Byron stood immobile on the ledge. Rustom fired at him. Apparently hit, the cat opened his mouth, flailed the air with his paws and fell on his back.

Boulos' face regained some color, his eyes started to blink. He looked around, finally fixing his gaze on Rustom.

Once more, Rustom aimed the weapon at Byron. Boulos jumped from behind, grabbed Rustom's throat and dragged him to the floor. In spite of violent efforts to free himself, Rustom's face was starting to turn violet. His gun went off.

Blood covered Aziz's face and he slowly went down. Lynn took his gun.

Again, Rustom's hand went up in the air, his finger on the trigger. He would fire in her direction, but she calmly shot him in the chest.

Holding Boulos, she slowly reached the street.

"Poor Byron," she said, crying.

Vartkes was waiting for them in his cab. The Mercedes started to shake and bounce over the torn pavement. Suddenly, Vartkes stopped the taxi and stepped out to open the door. Like a small furry ghost covered with blood and dust, Byron limped in and took his place on the back seat.

The Cheat

Albert Goussin, seated at the Café Ondine, dipped the croissant into the black coffee and took a bite. The place was quiet except for the barman jingling empty glasses. Today there were no classes to teach, he could take his time. He opened the newspaper at the travel section and skimmed it for special rates for a trip he planned to take. He wished he could leave immediately. He had to admit . . . he was mentally and physically exhausted, but he still had the final exam to face.

Outside, the sun caressed the chestnut trees. It reminded him of the day they had buried Yvonne. Her memories still lived deep within him, becoming especially painful when he was alone in the house. His doctor had strongly encouraged a change of scene.

Someone opened the door, and he heard bits of an ongoing conversation between two young men. The voices sounded familiar. He even thought he heard one of them mention his name. Being seated in a remote corner, he pushed his wrought iron seat farther behind the column where he could observe without being noticed.

One boy, about seventeen, stared over the top of his metallic sunglasses, and surveyed the empty row of tables.

"Very easy to do," he said to the second boy who was still outside.

The first boy looked at his reflection in the glass and carefully combed his styled black hair. Goussin smiled. He had almost not recognized Antonin, who was one of his students, all decked out in a western shirt covered with sequins and wearing Rafisto sneakers.

The second boy came in. It was Jules Lenoir, another of his students.

"I'm not sure this is where we should be discussing it," Jules said, looking around. "I've seen Goussin in here once or twice."

Goussin hunched down in his chair, wondering in passing if Jules' father, policeman Lenoir, knew that his son spent time loitering around coffee shops. Jules seated himself at a table, across from Antonin. Goussin could only see his back.

The barman came over and took their orders. The boys waited a while before resuming their conversation.

"Are you still trying to get me to trick Goussin into giving you a make-up exam?" Jules finally said, nervously passing his fingers over his close cropped blond hair as his friend opened a comics magazine and started to skim through it.

"It'll be an adventure," Antonin said.

"You had your fun, playing around instead of studying for the final," Jules said. "Am I now supposed to get your derrière out of the fire?"

"Yes, but what a thrill," Antonin said, as he continued to leaf through the magazine.

"To tell you the truth, I don't see much thrill in your plan."

Antonin closed the magazine, thought for a while then looked his friend in the eye.

"No, I guess it wouldn't thrill you," he said. "But imagine yourself as a modern Prince Valiant, dashing out to help a companion in need."

"Blah-blah-blah."

"It'll be good," Antonin said. "Afterwards, we'll both remember it and laugh."

"Hah, I'm laughing already," Jules said. "This old song is getting pretty tiresome."

The barman brought over cafés au lait and vanilla éclairs for two.

"Delicious," Antonin said, biting into a pastry. "How do you like it?"

Jules nodded.

"It's all on me, friend," Antonin said and put his hand on Jules' shoulder. "Now will you do it?"

Jules thought about the question.

"And there's little risk involved?" Jules said.

"I'll take care of everything."

There was another silence from Jules. Antonin looked at him with insistence, expecting an answer.

"Well, okay I guess," Jules said.

Antonin smiled and shook his hand several times.

Goussin waited a while for the boys to leave, and stood up to pay. Something he'd just read in the paper came back to him.

"The fish are biting in Ibiza," he said to himself.

Goussin looked around the classroom. It was filled with students busily writing down answers on notebooks of ruled paper. In another hour and a half, the fastest among them would start handing in their completed papers, while the exam itself would end half an hour after that.

Then, all the way from the other side of the room, someone called for "M'sieur Goussin!". He looked in that direction and recognized the sequined shirt and Rafisto sneakers. Antonin's face exuded pain as he held on to his stomach and whispered to him. Goussin nodded, and called for the school secretary to accompany the boy to the restroom.

The hands on the wall clock continued their round for a few minutes. Antonin returned to his seat and began to work on the exam. The clock hands raced some more, then the boy called

Goussin once more, again to complain about a colic. The teacher looked at the boy's face. His pupils were dilated and his skin sweaty. Goussin called the school nurse.

Upon her arrival, the beads of sweat on Antonin's forehead seemed to grow larger.

"This may be due to a virus or even some stress, who knows?" Goussin said in a comforting tone. "At any rate, I hope it's nothing serious."

The expression of grief on Antonin's face increased as the hefty nurse pushed him in the direction of the infirmary.

"Lucky for you that doctor Taille is in today," she said. "He is *very* thorough and will find out what's wrong."

Antonin made a very sick sound.

It was nine o'clock of the following morning. Goussin was in his office and watched as a shadow fluttered across the frosted glass door.

"Jules?" he said.

The boy came in. For someone his generation, his clothes looked ordinary. He wore a pair of khaki slacks, a white shirt and regular three hole brown shoes.

The teacher glanced at the opposite side of the room, where two windows let the pale light come in: it was going to be another cloudy day in this suburb of Paris. Jules sat in one of the two old chairs facing his wooden desk. A moment later, Antonin walked in.

"Morning," Goussin said.

He tried to hide a smile. Two days had passed, but Antonin still carried a pained expression on his face. Goussin deliberately pulled a crumpled handkerchief from his back pocket and cleaned his eyeglasses. He put them back on his nose and looked at the boys seated in front of him.

"My friends," he said, "I am a very unhappy man. I was hoping that the colic that Antonin experienced during the final was just a passing thing, a quirk of nature."

He looked at Jules.

"But now it seems that you had something to do with it?"

"Me, monsieur? What have I done?"

The teacher cleared his throat.

"Would you mind answering a few questions?" he said.

"Of course."

"The morning of the exam, what time did you come to school?"

Jules said that it was an important final, scheduled to start at eight, and that he wanted to make sure he was on time. He was in the school yard around seven-thirty. A number of students were already there, waiting.

"Did you talk to anyone?"

"Antonin."

"About what?"

"He complained about some hoarseness in his throat."

Antonin's face turned crimson, as he started to stir in his chair. With repeated gestures of his right hand, Goussin ordered him to be quiet.

He strolled across the room, and stopped near a window. There was a clear spot on the glass created by the rain of the night before. Through it, he saw that the fog was getting denser.

He imagined that at this moment, off the coast of Spain, fishing boats were leaving with the tide. He could smell new paint on the old hull, hear the wood creaking, and feel the force of the wind whipping the sail. Soon, he would be standing on that deck, carefully choosing a live sardine and piercing its wriggling body with a steel hook. Meanwhile, unaffected by the heaving waves, the captain stood erect, reading the current. He looked solemnly around him, then raised his hand. Not yet, his gesture meant, this was not a good spot. The fish schools were a bit further away. Just a few more minutes and they'd be there. The captain then came to him, smiled, and handed him a wine flask made of rough leather.

"Salud."

"Too early in the morning," Goussin said.

There was an amused giggle.

". . . too early, monsieur?" Jules said.

The teacher saw his face mirrored in the pane, and was startled to recognize the round features, thinning black hair and the glasses with large circular rims. The man that looked back at him with half shut eyelids had been lost in a faraway dream.

He turned around to face Jules.

"... I meant to say, that the day of the final, early in the morning, everybody was somewhat nervous. That is perfectly normal. You say that Antonin's voice was hoarse. Did you offer him anything, maybe some food or refreshment, to help him out?"

"I gave him a mint candy."

"Poisoned candy is what he gave me," Antonin said, as if preparing to pounce on Jules.

Still seated, Jules moved his body away a little. The teacher grabbed Antonin by the shoulders, and forced him back in the chair.

"Gentlemen, gentlemen, please!" he shouted, forcefully pounding his desk and tipping a glass ball he used as a paperweight. The ball slowly started to roll toward the edge. He caught it, put it back with care, and watched the animated scene inside, as the snow fell over the quiet village.

"Now, about that candy, Jules?" he said after

a while. "Do you recall specifically what type it was?"

"It was an Altoid. My favorite mint."

"Where did it come from?"

"From the Cowboy stand. Across the street."

Goussin scratched the bald spot in back of his head with the middle finger of his right hand.

He looked at Jules. "Antonin says that he had been in good health the days before the exam, and that he had eaten breakfast together with his family that morning. No one had complained about any illness. It looks very likely that his colic was caused by the bonbon you gave him."

Jules looked at his feet, then at Antonin who was staring out the window.

"Jules Lenoir," the teacher said, "do you have anything to say?"

The boy continued to look out the window.

"Look, you two . . . I don't have much time for charades, but I was at the Café Ondine and heard you discuss your little plot. Then afterwards, I figured out how you did it."

The two boys looked at each other in amazement.

"Yes, I was there the whole time," he said, "seated behind a column. I don't think it's very funny. I want you to convince me why I should not ask the principal to send each of you a letter of eviction from the lycée."

Antonin was the first to recover.

"Eviction? You must be joking," he said. "Just remember who my dad is, president of the Banque Paysanne. All he has to do is make one phone call, and the principal will forget about sending any such letter."

Antonin got up, said "Good day, monsieur," and left.

Jules, who had been silent throughout the exchange, looked at Goussin.

"Antonin's father is rich," he said, "and my dad only works for the City Police, so he has no influence."

Goussin listened as the boy went on . . . "Antonin convinced me to go along with his scheme, and act as if I had given him a mint laced with Ex-Lax. According to the plan, you would put the blame on me and give Antonin a make-up exam. Thus, he would be allowed enough time to prepare."

"Anything else?"

"Yes, I am sorry to have taken part in this deception. Truly sorry, monsieur. Please do not throw me out of school."

"What you have done is very bad. But you have confessed, and I will, for the time being, forget about the expulsion. But at the least sign of further malfeasance, you're out for good."

"Thank you, monsieur. You will never have any reason to be unhappy with me."

After Jules' departure, Goussin decided to go home. It was getting late and he had to finish packing.

The only missing item he needed to take along was his fishing rod, which he had forgotten at the office. The next morning, he made a quick trip there to pick it up.

To his surprise, he saw that Antonin was waiting for him. The boy asked if he had heard the news. He said he had not.

"It was certainly unexpected. Bad scene alto-gether," Antonin said. "I guess what it means is that from now on, I'm going to have to change my ways."

"Speaking in general," Goussin said, "I agree it's a good idea. But would you mind explaining what you're talking about?"

"My dad's company, Banque Paysanne, de-clared bankruptcy last night. Rather bad timing, I'd say."

"I am sorry," Goussin said, trying to put a serious expression on his face.

"Please forgive me for what I said yesterday. I hope that Jules will forgive me too. It was too easy, he is just the type who will do anything I say."

"Not any more," Goussin said. "There is one point that still puzzles me."

"Yes, monsieur?"

"I have been officially informed by doctor Taille that you had a colic caused by ingestion of a laxative. But according to my information, didn't your plan only call for you to *fake* a colic?"

Antonin looked embarrassed.

"I did not expect the nurse to take me to see doctor Taille," he said looking at his Rafistos. "On my way to the infirmary, I frantically searched through my pockets. Lucky for me, I found a real Ex-Lax tablet and took it."

The teacher shook his head.

"And by the time you reached the doctor, your colic was for real."

Antonin nodded.

The teacher was forced to smile.

"I know that from now on, my situation is changed, and so is my attitude," Antonin said. "Please do not expel me from school. I want to take the exam over."

"Had you come to me with such words yesterday," Goussin said, "I would have tried to fix things. But I am about to go on a vacation, one that I need badly."

"Has the principal already decided to dismiss me?"

"He hasn't told me," the teacher said.

"Is this what you want? Expel me permanently from school?"

Goussin scratched his chin.

"Yesterday, my main concern was whether I was going to condone cheating during exams," he said. "Was I going to allow you to cheat, because you have influential parents? After you told me that the possibility of a dismissal was of little concern to you, I sent in such a request, just to see what would happen."

"People make mistakes," Antonin said, "especially at my young age. I have recognized my wrongdoing and apologized to everybody. What good could possibly come from expelling me?"

The boy sounded very serious. Goussin went to the window, mulling the question.

"I think of you as a gifted young man who has up till now wasted his talent," he said, making sure the pane was secure. "I agree that your expulsion is not going to produce much good."

"Then will you let me take the exam over?"

Goussin stared at him in silence. He lowered the venetian blinds and wondered whether Antonin deserved more help than another, more average student. Goussin could either put his own interest first and go on the trip, or help Antonin and stay over.

Trying to make up his mind, he took the fishing rod and walked onto the schoolyard, Antonin trotting behind him. Looking across the large empty space, he noticed the cracks and multicolored blemishes on the gray concrete walls of the school building. The large windows looked back at him through dusty glasses, and reminded him of all the classrooms he had lectured in. There was one pane near the far end of the building that had a hole that was not yet repaired. He must have told the janitor about it a thousand times. He also noticed that other room, where in answer to a boy's stupid question, he threw the chalk eraser against the window, the milky outlines of the little rectangle were still visible on the glass.

Goussin looked over his shoulder, and saw that Antonin was still following.

"Will you, monsieur Goussin? Will you?" Antonin asked.

"The fish are biting in Ibiza," Goussin said and continued walking.

The Inquisition

For weeks, Rayne had been afraid to go there. She had finally worked up the courage and now stood in a long line. Maybe she could catch the midnight show.

The smiling hunk in front of her tried to start a conversation. She nodded politely, not wanting to get involved.

Someone pushed her from behind. The hunk turned and shoved his elbow against her breast.

"Hell," she said.

Same as in the subway, she couldn't tell whether he was trying to feel her up or what. She backed away to give him room.

"Fight . . . fight . . ." somebody yelled. People ran to see what was happening, but she didn't move. She had no one to hold her place and was afraid there might be shooting.

Now that some of the crowd had drifted away to watch the fight, she was able to see the building. Still the same cube of lead colored stucco. A massive ironware torch spewed a yellow gas flame which threw dancing shadows against the wall. A blue neon sign spelled out the words: "The Inquisition."

Suddenly, out of the front door, a midget raced toward the fight. His hands and feet were small, but he had a thick, powerful neck and bulging biceps. He carried a stiletto in his belt.

She shrank away, not wanting him to notice her. She knew him well. He was the bouncer.

"Shiv is coming," voices cried out, and the commotion ended.

Shiv turned and walked slowly back, casting a malevolent look out of his one good eye. Rayne made herself even smaller.

"Afraid o' de bozo?" the hunk said. "Don't be, I'll take care of him."

Uneasily, Rayne shook her head. This man didn't know Shiv like she knew him.

The hunk flashed his teeth and leered at her breasts pressing against her dress. She blushed and turned away. He made her feel like a piece of meat. She wished she was tall and willowy.

A long-haired guy in a rainbow bandanna, checked ID's at the door. His breath stank of Mary Jane. She coughed and moved on. All she wanted was to see Pep.

Once inside, she was assaulted by the smell of stale beer and cigarettes. Her eyes took a while to see through the smoke. She was in the big room, the one with the black walls and the ceiling painted the color of blood. And the tables, the size of postcards with just enough room for a candle in a red glass, with a little left over to hold drinks. The chairs were very small and adults could only sit half-moon style.

On the lit-up wall behind the bandstand, was a large painting of a man, face contorted in pain, being pulled apart on a rack. Below the picture, someone had lettered: "The Inquisition."

In the flickering light of candles, chains could be seen held by rods against the walls. Whips and a large iron bed hung from the high ceiling.

Rayne spotted one of the few empty tables and sat down. Her mind drifted. She was interrupted by a waitress in black leotards, jet-black hair and a ring in her pierced nose.

"Drink?"

Rayne looked up at the tired face. Thought for a moment.

"Fruit punch," she said.

The waitress showed no reaction.

"Fruit punch," Rayne shouted over the music.

The waitress nodded her head and walked away.

Five minutes later her drink came. She paid four dollars. She would have to nurse the fruit punch. Her purse was nearly empty.

Her mind chilled out, went into memory. There was that time . . . it now seemed so long ago. She was in her glory days as the lead singer of Pandemonium and in love with Pep. But she was feeling burned out and asked Gunther for two weeks off. "Hell," he'd said, "we can't spare you, doll." Then he said he had something that would make her feel better. She wanted to say no, but she was feeling a deep blue and she thought, only once how can it hurt? But she came back for more and more and one day he wouldn't give her any unless she rolled over for him. God, she loved Pep, but she rolled over for Gunther every night before she went on. And one day she found herself pregnant with Gunther's kid and she couldn't go through with it, not with Gunther's kid, a kid with junk in its blood. So she'd had herself fixed and she rolled into deep blackness, knowing she could no longer help herself. She left town. There was this clinic . . . months of sweat and shaking . . . group sessions. They brought her back from the dead. Now she had to see Pep. Did he still love her? Could she come back to a career with him? But not here. Not at The Inquisition.

She was brought back to reality by the sound of loud guitars. The opening act was on. Pretty awful. Three long-haired youths who called themselves the Hog Wilds, strummed their Fenders as loud as possible, "A-tumma . . . A-tumma . . . A-tumma," heavy on the metal but light on the harmony.

Some guys began to mimic them.

"A-tumma . . . A-tumma . . . A-tumma."

The Hog Wilds paid no attention.

In the front of the room, teenagers started to mosh, passing a girl down on raised hands. Others clapped and danced.

Some people will dance to anything, Rayne thought.

To enlarge the mosh pit, the teens tried to push some of the tables out of the way. An argument started.

A fat girl threw a plastic cup of beer at the moshers and missed. Her projectile arced toward the stage hitting the lead Hog right between the eyes. He gasped, wiped his face, and went after her.

"A sister's being attacked," other girls screamed. "Go after the cahones."

"Fight, fight . . ." the audience chanted.

A table landed against the bandstand wall, barely missing the face of the man in the painting. The table shattered.

A second Hog went to help his leader, who was being held down by the girls. A serving tray landed on his head. Rayne ducked under her table.

"Ladies and gentlemen," a voice boomed out of the powerful speaker system, "the band you've been waiting for! Welcome Pandemonium."

The brawl ended. The klieg lights focused on three smiling young men in ruby red costumes. The lead guitar, the drummer, and an electric bass played, "I Loved You Last Night." The audience swayed to the music, and moved their arms from side to side.

Suddenly, a young man jumped on stage. Waves of brown hair flowed down his back. He was barefoot and only wore trousers held up by a wide leather belt. At the sight of his suntanned muscles, women cried out hysterically: "Pep . . . Pep . . . Pep . . ."

One of them fainted and was carried out.

Pep grabbed the mike and sang:

"In the dawn when buildings wake
    I go looking for you
    I ask you for my sake
To come back, to come back, to come back."

Hearing the words, Rayne began to cry and

hid her face in her hands. When she finally looked up, Pep had grabbed his electric guitar and was grooving with the rest of the group. After several numbers, each one greeted by wild applause, the band took a fifteen minute break.

Rayne elbowed her way toward the stage, but could not reach Pep who was surrounded by a gaggle of girls. One wanted his autograph on a program, another on a book, a third just wanted a kiss.

The redhead in front asked him to write a few words on her leg cast. As he doodled on the plaster, he looked at the next person in line and his face lit up.

"Rayne!" he said.

The clamor for autographs continued.

"No more," he said. He took Rayne's hand and led her behind the stage, to a large area filled with old music stands, several broken guitars, rolls of dusty backdrops and heavy electrical cables. Among the empty boxes, there were several tables equipped with makeup lights. One of them was his.

He took her hands and pulled her toward

him. Waves undulated down her body. She felt weak.

"Baby, baby," he said, "I've been looking for you for five long months. Where the hell have you been?"

She turned away. He took her shoulders gently and looked into her eyes.

"You can tell me," he said.

"Couldn't you tell? I was on junk. Went to this expensive clinic for detox."

"No, you hid it good. Why didn't you tell me?"

She shook her head.

"My head felt like a pre-amp getting too much feedback and I loved you too much to let you see me like I was."

"God, I hope you've licked it."

A techie gave Pep a signal. Pandemonium was back on. Pep pulled her against him and gave her a long kiss.

"Meet me here after the set. We have a lot to talk about."

She looked at herself in the large mirror. There was a hint of rings under her eyes. She rummaged through her purse for some make-up.

She glanced back at the mirror, and drew back in horror. A face with one good eye was grinning back at her.

"Why, if t'ain't Sweet Lips," Shiv joked. "What you doing 'ere?"

It took her a few seconds to regain her breath.

"Can't you see, I'm powdering my nose."

"Pretty snippy, girl. Don't shu know? There's a certain person real eager t'see ya again."

"Gunther? I'm not eager to see him." She started to leave.

"No, yer don't."

He blocked her way and his lips curled down.

"There's someone I have to meet," she pleaded.

"If you mean Pep, ferget it. Move."

They took a long, dark corridor. In the background, she heard the audience break out in loud applause.

They stopped at a large door made of imitation oak. It said: "Grand Inquisitor." Shiv tapped.

Gunther hadn't changed much, he was a little heavier, but it was hard to tell. His body went to fat anyway, all six foot two of him. Rayne remembered how he used to slobber over her like a St. Bernard. Her stomach cramped.

Gunther was totally absorbed by what was happening on a screen placed on his desk.

"Didn't I tell ya I want to be left alone— important business." he said, his gaze still fixed on the set. "Boy, this 'Roxie Does The Redskins' is prime porn. Not only does she tackle the whole team, but she also does the Redskinettes. What a mouth on this gal!"

He looked back and noticed Rayne, standing there with Shiv.

"Sweetie," he said. He motioned for Shiv to go. "Is it true you were going to leave town without even saying hello to your old boyfriend?"

She felt like a tarantula had just slithered down her back.

"Sorry, Gunther. I was in a hurry."

"Seat yourself and have something. Mm . . . you got no idea how much I missed you. Your public, they want you back, doll, and so do I."

Gunther gestured toward a gold Regency chair. She hesitated but decided to sit down.

"Much better," he said, ". . . some bubbly?"

She shrugged. He pulled a chilled bottle of Moët et Chandon from his refrigerator and poured for both. He lit a group of red candles hanging on a chandelier and killed the electric lights. The room was enveloped in a shadowy, warm glow.

She was frightened, but decided to play along. Shiv might be just outside the door.

"Chin-chin," Gunther said as their glasses touched. "To my one and only."

"Oh, c'mon, you got plenty of other women."

"You know my problem," he said as he gestured with his glass. "You're the only one who can help me get it up . . . Say, Sweetie, how'd you like a little Beam Me Up? Got some fresh stuff just came in."

"No, Gunther," she said. "You got me on junk before, and you had me begging like a dog for more. You wouldn't give me any till I rolled over for you. Well, I'm not doing that anymore."

She rose from her chair.

"I know, I know. All I ask is that you come back to work for me. No strings."

"I hate to take the chance."

"Hey, let's have a little champagne to toast the old times."

"And then I could go?" she said, a note of hope clinging to her voice.

"Sure, why not?" He smiled at her.

She sipped the cold Moët. In the distance, she thought she heard the whistles and the shouts begging Pandemonium to come back. She heard Pep's voice working the crowd and the band played again. She knew it would be their last number. She worried about what Pep would do when he didn't find her.

Her eyelids began to close. Strange, she had had enough sleep. Maybe the drink, she thought. She hadn't had one in a long time. The lights flitted like butterflies. Her eyes wouldn't focus. Gunther's voice grew distant. She tried to get up but fell back into the chair. She didn't know how long she was out.

From deep somewhere she was jolted into a half awake state by Gunther helping her rise.

"I have a surprise for you," he said as he led

her to the main room which was now deserted. He sat her on one of the small chairs and bowed to her.

"My queen," he said.

He waddled to a switch on the wall. A motor started to hum and the massive iron bed descended from the ceiling.

"I've got something for you to lie on," he said.

She lay down on the bed. She didn't feel the hardness of the metal springs. Everything in her yearned for sleep.

Out of a medieval trunk set against the wall, he took a ruby-studded dog collar. The anticipation made his eyes sparkle. His loose skin dripped with beads of sweat.

He grabbed her dress and ripped it open. After admiring her nude breasts, he lovingly placed the collar on her neck.

He shackled her wrists to the railing at the head of the bed and tied her legs to the other side of the bed.

"Help!" her numb brain cried out, but her mouth made no sound.

He teased her with the whip. Suddenly, he

lashed out, leaving three distinct trails of blood across her breasts. He whipped her once more across the belly.

The pain woke her completely. She writhed against the shackles and gritted her teeth to keep from crying out. She knew that if she screamed, he'd whip her again.

"Party time," he said. "But first, we need a shot of Beam Me Up."

"No," she cried out. "It took me months to get clean."

"Such a shame it only takes one hit to get dirty. Ain't life a bitch?"

From his pocket, he pulled out two syringes.

"First me and then you."

He rolled up the sleeve on his fat arm and pushed in the needle. His eyes rolled and he smiled. He sat down and waited for the feeling to start.

Rayne shivered. She couldn't believe she was getting aroused.

"Your turn, sweetie," he said as he grabbed her arm and raised the syringe.

"Wait," she cried out. "Kiss me first."

"Granted."

He lay the syringe down on the table and bent over. She looped the chain of her shackles around his neck and pulled tight. His eyes started to bulge.

"Unlock me," she said.

He shook his head. She gave the chain another twist.

He pulled out the key and threw it on the bed. His eyes begged for her to let him go. She kept up her choke hold until he passed out.

She unfastened her hands and legs, then shackled him to the iron bed. She lifted his head, and slapped him across the face. Gunther groaned and opened his eyes.

The outside door opened. A man's silhouette appeared against the blinking neon lights. She raised the whip, ready to take him on.

"It's me."

She recognized Pep's voice and threw the whip away.

Pep looked around the room. "What happened here?" he said. She told him.

"I'm so sorry," he said. He led her to the door. They opened it but had to stop. Shiv stood there, stiletto in hand.

"Whatsa matter? Need fresh air. Not yet, the boss didn't say I let'shu go." He pointed with his blade back toward the room.

"So she likes him better than me?" Gunther said. "Cut off his balls."

"In front of the lady?" Shiv's one good eye lit up.

"Yeah, let her watch."

Shiv took several steps toward Pep. Rayne backed up toward the wall. She pulled the switch. The room went dark.

She got down on her hands and knees, and explored the floor. She hoped to find the whip. Her fingers touched the medieval trunk. Fear wet her armpits as she rummaged through it, looking for a weapon. Everything in the trunk felt like leather garments.

"Where'you hidin', good-looking boy?" Shiv said.

The sound of quick steps echoed through the room.

"Oooy—" Shiv said as he tripped over something. "Now I gotcha, me boy."

"Help me," Pep said, "this guy's too strong."

"Snip-snip," Shiv said.

Rayne turned the light on. In the center of the room, Pep was on his back. Shiv sat on top of him, grasping at his wide belt with his left hand. With a jab from his stiletto, Shiv cut the belt and pulled Pep's pants down.

"Go ahead, cut off the family jewels," Gunther cheered on.

The dwarf grabbed at Pep's jockey shorts.

Rayne dumped the contents of the trunk, picked it up and swung it several times against Shiv's head.

Shiv lay unconscious and bloody. Pep freed himself and took the stiletto from his hand. Rayne kept hitting Shiv's head.

"Enough," said Pep as he grabbed the bloody trunk from her hands. "He's out." He picked up Shiv and flung him on the bed. Rayne shackled him next to Gunther.

She hit the switch and with a soft whir, the

bed rose and locked itself and its cargo against the ceiling.

She found a plastic table cloth, wrapped it around herself and tied the ends so it would stay. It felt cold against her skin.

Pep was still in his jockey shorts.

"You can't go out like this," she told him. Among the contents of the trunk that were scattered on the floor, she found a small belt. Pep used it to fasten his pants.

"I'll get you for this," Gunther screamed down from the ceiling. "No one crosses the Grand Inquisitor. No one . . ."

The lovers went out into the night air. The neon sign blinked on and off. There was a full moon and several stars twinkled in the cold night sky.

"How'd you happen to come back?" Rayne said.

"At first, I thought you'd blown me off, so I hit the highway. But I kept having this feeling that something was wrong."

She kissed him on the cheek.

"I'll never thank you enough for whacking the dwarf with that trunk," he said.

They got into his old Chevy van and took off for the highway. Few cars were on the road that late, maybe graveyard shifters on their way home.

"I still can't shake myself out of it," she said after a while, rubbing her eyes.

"Yeah, rough night."

"What bothers me is that after he hit me with the whip, and waved that needle around, I felt turned on. Can you imagine? Turned on! What's wrong with me? "

Pep patted her on the back.

"Don't let it worry you. When it comes to sex, we humans are the strangest animals around."

She sighed. It was still night, the world was bathed in the bleak light of mercury lamps. The linear road, green exit signs and painted traffic lanes went on and on. In spite of the pain, she placed her weary head on Pep's chest.

"Sing to me," she said.

Death Row Follies

"Get up, get up," a man's voice said in the dark.

Josh Adley groaned in his sleep and tried to say something. All that came up was a sick cough. The voice came back, insistent.

"C'mon, Adley, get up."

The tube in the ceiling flashed, died, and came on. He covered his eyes with one hand and looked around the narrow cell. In addition to the man who was trying to wake him up, there were four guards, their twelve gauge shotguns at the ready. With an unsteady gait, he reached the metal commode and took a pee. It left a strong stink, even after he flushed it down.

He turned back and saw a tray of food. He sat on the metal bed and poured coffee into a plastic cup. It was hot, black and fragrant. He started to munch on the sausage and eggs, trying to guess what time it was. The cell had no window, and the only noise he could hear was the steady hum of the ventilation system.

He turned the electric shaver on. The motor buzzed and protested as it massaged his skin. The long hairs stubbornly refused to be cut. The tiny mirror on the wall reflected the features of a grown man, with dark stubble growing from his pale skin. Small ridges around his mouth and eyes made him look older.

When he was done, they clicked handcuffs on him and placed manacles on his feet. Then they marched him through a long corridor, to an unoccupied cell block, and stopped in front of a gray metal door.

The head guard knocked twice and said: "Prisoner Adley."

Someone on the other side worked some heavy bars and opened the door.

"Yes?" a uniformed man with a black mustache said.

"We bring the first one, Adley."

The man looked the prisoner over and said: "Check. I'll take it from here."

He guided Josh in and elaborately locked the door, leaving the others out.

The room had no windows, and the smell of stale tobacco hung everywhere. The guard sat him down on a metal chair and attached his manacled feet to it.

"You right-handed?"

"Yes."

Opening a rectangular case which contained a collection of square bladed swords with long wooden handles, he selected one and placed it in a wooden scabbard.

"Now," the guard said, as he undid the handcuffs. "I'm gonna hand you the sword."

Josh nodded.

"See how it feels in both hands. And don't get stupid," the guard said as he took out his gun. "Ready?"

"Yes."

He pulled out the steel blade and waved it back and forth in one hand, then the other.

"OK?" the guard said.

"Yes."

The guard took back the sword and placed it

in its sheath. A loud buzzer sounded once. The guard looked at his wristwatch. The other door in the room opened, and through it entered two armed guards. One of them unfastened Josh's feet from the chair and handed him a round metal shield.

"You'll need this."

The buzzer went off twice. At the signal, the two guards took him into another small room. Through a half open door, gray light poured in, too much for his eyes accustomed to darkness, so he looked the other way. While they waited, one guard took two ten inch squares of white linen. They were marked with the number "72." The man patted a square so its velcro attached itself to the front of Josh's gray T-shirt, and attached the other square to the back.

The buzzer went off three times.

"You're on," a guard said, giving him the sword and pointing him to the door. Before he stepped out, he turned to the guard.

"How many rounds to this thing?"

"Till the end."

"The end," he repeated and slowly walked out.

He found himself in a cage of steel, some thirty by thirty yards in size. There was no way to escape this animal pen.

A number of lights came on, illuminating a runway that surrounded the cage on three sides. He heard loud cat calls from the audience as a well stacked Wonder Woman strutted her stuff the length of the runway and back, holding a sign that read: "Round One."

There were elegant sky boxes all around the perimeter. The sky box closest to him was occupied by a distinguished-looking gentleman in his early eighties, dressed in a burgundy colored dinner jacket, matching bow tie and pants, and a pink shirt with ruffles. He sat next to a man in his late twenties with a Malibu tan wearing a black dinner jacket and pants, white shirt and black tie. An elderly waiter came in with a tray, and distributed long stem glasses filled with sparkling champagne. If there was anything to suggest a father and son scene, it was soon dispelled by the sensual way the two men kissed each other.

Looming high against the dark sky, an electronic score board came alive. It showed his name in lights, 'No. 72 ADLEY vs. No. 277 BURSCHT.' Underneath the names, numbers came on and started to change. Finally, the board read:

"ODDS

1-10   10-1."

The old gentleman in the sky box carefully studied the data on a screen and made a hurried call.

A powerful set of spot lights came on and covered the center of the cage. On the opposite side, he saw a gate come open with a loud series of bangs. Silence fell and along with everyone in the place, he looked at his opponent's gate. A powerfully built figure showed up, nimbly moving his six foot seven body around.

Josh checked his grip on the sword. He'd heard of Burscht before, the inmate with a toddler's brain and a mountain of muscle.

For the moment, Burscht moved around the cage like a wild animal surveying his territory. The number on Burscht's T-shirt was '277,' and could have been a reference to his weight. The sudden clanging of the gate made him jump. He carried the sword in his right hand. Compared to this giant, Adley at a hundred and ninety-five pounds felt puny.

The buzzer sounded once more. Burscht started to yell: "Sieg, Sieg, Sieg," and marched triumphantly to the center of the cage, his shoulder length blond hair flowing behind him. Slowly, his gaze swept the audience. When he stopped, he brandished the sword and broke the blade against his leg.

Like everyone in the audience, the move caught Josh unawares. Quickly, the giant ran in his direction. He looked for a way to retreat, but the giant was soon upon him, almost pinning him to the fence. Josh straightened his shield and pointed his sword toward his opponent. Burscht stopped and fixed him with steely blue eyes while undulating his shoulders from side to side. Swiftly, he turned around. His left foot connected with the sword and kicked it away.

The giant let out a roar and was on Josh. Smelling like an animal, he pounded his thick elbows against Josh's ribs. His arms found their aim on his stomach and the back of his shoulders. As the blows rained on his head, Josh used the shield to cover himself, only to make his opponent angrier. The giant pounded on the metal, and bent it in places. Then Josh started to see stars everywhere.

Outside the fence, guards hurried to spray them with powerful jets of icy water as the buzzer sounded to announce a short rest period.

"Fighters, move to your corners," the sound from a powerful speaker ordered. "Now."

Looking disappointed, Burscht slowly walked over to his corner. With difficulty, Josh straightened himself up, took his sword and regained his corner. A guard placed a wet towel on his head, which revived him somewhat.

"The fight resumes in one minute," the voice in the loudspeaker announced.

His eyes ran to the electronic board. After

his poor showing in the first round, his chances of winning had slipped to one in twenty five.

The older man in the sky box placed a call. The buzzer sounded, and Wonder Woman made her appearance to announce "Round Two."

Once more Josh found himself on his feet, shield deployed and pointing his sword forward. Burscht came running, but stopped some eight feet away. The giant turned his body to the right and sent his right foot back in the direction of Josh's sword. Josh moved his weapon up behind his head and quickly made a forward up-down arc with it. Burscht grabbed his right side with his hand and looked at his palm. It was bloody.

The giant looked at Josh, and the muscles in his face contorted into an ugly smirk. He turned back and moved five feet away. Rapidly bending over, he touched the ground with both hands and executed a swift back kick aiming his feet at Josh. The left foot found Josh's blade and sent it through the air. Josh heard the metal hit the fence behind him. Giant arms surrounded his head and, like a vise, started to press on it. The bones in his head felt as if they were about to crack. The intense pain made him whimper. He was about to pass out.

He heard the giant emit a victory yell, and the huge arms moved down to his rib cage. He felt like an athlete who had the wind knocked out of him. With what little strength he had, he kicked the giant in the crotch, until the giant began to let go. The huge hands grabbed at his own mid section. His cry increased as he started to go down. A shot of ice water surprised both fighters.

This time, there was no need for the guards to separate the opponents. Each headed off to a corner. Josh touched his chest. He could hardly breathe, and suspected that he had some cracked ribs. The board now gave him one chance in fifteen.

Wonder Woman strutted by, and announced "Round Three."

With difficulty, Josh grabbed onto his shield and found his sword. Burscht approached, and tried the same back flip. Josh placed his shield in the way and the giant's feet connected with it. The impact threw Josh two feet back. The giant moved close and tried to grab Josh by his prison shirt. Josh lunged forward with his sword. The metal penetrated the giant's sternum. Burscht loudly called for his mother. He cried, grabbed his chest and slowly sank to his knees. Blood poured out of the gash, and he fell face first to the ground. He started to shiver. He opened his mouth, tried to say something and died.

The fight was over. His chest felt like it was made of razor blades. A prison doctor came in.

"Looks like we have some serious fractures," the doc said as he applied a wide tape. "I'll be able to tell you more after I see some x-rays."

Four guards escorted Josh to the prison infirmary. A radiology technician asked him to lie down on a large cold surface and got busy adjusting his equipment.

"Don't breathe."

"For me, that's easy to do."

"What?"

"Never mind."

The guards took him back to his cell. He never thought it possible, but at that moment he enjoyed seeing that place again. The guards carefully helped seat him on his bunk. One of them brought him a cream-colored cake with one candle on top and gave him a plastic knife with which to cut it. As the guard touched a match to the candle, Josh noticed the writing on top of the cake. It said: "FROM THE WARDEN."

"This for me?" he asked.

"The warden sends his wishes," the guard said.

Josh cut himself a slice. Inside, there was chocolate, sweet and gooey.

The guard switched some entertainment on for him. There was a game show in Spanish. The host was interviewing a fake blonde with big boobs who answered with dramatic gestures of her hands. Every time she said something, she'd wiggle her ass, and the audience would go wild. Josh laughed, but it was painful. He thought of switching to another channel, but instead turned his attention to the cake.

After a while, he felt tired and went to sleep.

He opened his eyes and saw that someone

had turned on the light in the cell. Four armed guards stood there.

"Enjoy the cake?" one of them asked.

"... yeah, very nice. What's up?"

There was no reply. One guard helped him get up while another one put shackles on him.

"Oh," Josh said, "in case you haven't heard, I won the fight."

There was silence.

"Where are you taking me? I had a deal with the warden."

The guards looked at each other and smiled.

"Way I hear it," one of the guards finally said, "you're not exactly the man of the moment. Some of the governor's buddies bet on your opponent and are out large sums of money."

"Where—where you guys taking me?"

He protested again. The warden had promised. If he won, the governor would commute his death sentence.

"Nice and quiet now," the head guard replied, pushing him forward. "We don't wanna disturb your buddies, do we?"

The Long Wait

The afternoon traffic crawled onto the three outbound lanes of the Nixon Memorial Bridge. Fred Zale, an unlit White Owl cigar hanging from his lip, was driving a brown Dodge van down the center lane, and mumbling to himself: "I don't like to drive in this area, it gives me the willies. But a job is a job."

Out of nowhere, the guy in the rusty-colored Honda up ahead, decided to slam on his brakes and bring his vehicle to a panic stop. Fred floored his brake pedal, stopping the car just inches from the little import in a squeal of rubber. His violent body reaction sent the White Owl flying. His brake started acting up, and felt under his foot like fresh-made dough. He applied his right foot in hopes of clearing any air bubble in the line, but in vain. A red "BRAKE" sign lit the dashboard.

"Oh please," he said, "don't do that now."

With his sleeve, he swabbed large drops of sweat from his brow. He maneuvered the van, which suddenly felt as heavy as a steam roller, and brought it to a stop in the breakdown lane. In front of him, two traffic cops were busy examining the scene of an accident. The burned-out shell of a Toyota Corolla was being loaded on a flat-bed truck. Even the windows of the wreck were smashed, as if by a violent explosion.

The cigar he lost in the excitement now rested, mangled, on the passenger seat. He fumbled in his breast pocket for a replacement, but found none. He grabbed his old cigar from the seat, and started it with a red and chrome lighter. He then hopped outside the van, and looked underneath for signs of damage. A dark circular oil puddle was starting to cover several square feet of road. Behind the right front wheel, oil was slowly seeping from the brake line. Checking under the hood, he noticed there was no oil left in the main brake cylinder.

He reached inside the van for a portable comm set, and called the Motor Club. His employer, Moore Technology, carried a corporate account with them. On the other end, a woman's voice said: "You may not know this, Sir, but *you are in a very bad area.* I am going to send you a tow truck as quickly as possible, within the next sixty minutes or so. Thank you for calling the Motor Club."

"A sixty-minute wait on a sunny day like this? What do you do during the winter snows? Wait for the arrival of spring?"

"I am sorry, Sir, but we've had a lot of calls today. Have a nice day." Click.

Earlier that afternoon, he had been called to his boss' office. Her name was Tawny Sparks, she was thirty-two, and had long white legs and shoulder-length black hair. He avoided looking up the black leather miniskirt she liked to hike. Having recently ended an unsuccessful Army career, he was not eager to be known here too as a trouble maker. Besides, he needed the paycheck.

"A big customer wants us to deliver a load of popular entertainment material, by tonight, to his warehouse on Stage Street. We're very busy right now, and all my other drivers are out making deliveries."

Fred approvingly nodded as she continued: "I told the client that I was temporarily unable to provide protection for the cargo, but he kept insisting. I can understand if you refuse to make the delivery under such conditions. But this is a very important customer, and we want to keep in his good graces." Propping herself up on her wingback chair, she whispered: "Make this delivery, and you will do me a favor I am not about to forget."

That was a couple of hours ago. Now he was stuck in a van with no brakes, on a long bridge filled with traffic, while an unhappy Tawny was saying: "Seven-thirty. Remember, we got to make this delivery by seven-thirty, or the customer walks."

He had another serious problem: "The equipment guys seem to have forgotten to give me the comm battery charger. The one battery I have is only three-quarters full."

At six-thirty, he decided to check back with the Motor Club. "I am sorry, Sir," the woman told him, "but we seem to have experienced a problem with your first call. We have a new computer system and frankly, it is a complete mess around here. Let me request a status check, and call you right back."

A cold wind was starting to blow. He stepped outside, and opened the back door of the van. Boxes marked "HyPelvent Storage Medium" were stacked three high along the walls. He found what he was looking for next to the merchandise, a blue metallic tool-box sitting on a greasy cotton blanket. A blanket could come in handy on a cold night. Inside the tool-box, amid an assortment of English and metric sockets, socket wrenches, triangular metal files and spark plugs, he found an L-shaped eighteen-inch tire-wrench. He wrapped the blanket around the tire-wrench, and brought the package back into the cabin. He hid it under his seat.

The operator at the Motor Club called back

at seven. "Sir, since you have been waiting patiently for hours in this really bad area, I am authorizing you to get help from any tow truck that may be out there. Just send us the bill for payment."

He thanked her, and admitted grudgingly to himself: "It's not her fault; the woman is doing her best."

The temperature in the van felt like it was near freezing. He started up the engine, to get some heat on his stiff limbs, and charge the car battery.

"Easy for her to say: get help from any tow truck," he said.

He decided to call his friend Bud, manager of the Newt Street Service Station, who answered in a scratchy voice: "Sure thing, Fred. I'll be drivin' the red tow truck. Dunno how long this' gonna take, but I'll see ya in a bit."

His mind took him back to the Army, and to Sergeant Fress. To chores mopping the floor, to mountains of potato peels, and midnight-to-sunrise guard duties.

"One night, I decided I'd had it up to here," he remembered.

Wearing black civvies and hiding in the bushes, his face concealed by a black ski mask, he waited patiently. At two in the morning, a drunken Fress showed up, all alone.

"Fress was in no condition to recognize me," he recalled. "I beat the stuffing out of him."

But soon enough, Fred learned that a number of phony insubordination charges were being brought up against him. In the end, it was his word against the sergeant's. And in this man's Army, it didn't take a rocket scientist to figure out the outcome. "I left my Army days behind, like a bad case of rash," he said, punctuating the statement with a spit of cigar residue.

Now it was dark on the bridge. Through the twin rear windows, he saw a beat-up full-size Chevy, slowly lumbering its way into the breakdown lane. One hundred feet away, the Chevy stopped. The driver, a powerfully built fellow, came out. The front passenger, a much smaller individual, extracted himself next. From the back of the vehicle, another man stepped out. He had a full head of frizzy hair that shimmered strangely in the pale light. The short passenger, a frisky customer, carefully buttoned a down jacket that was checkered with red and blue patches. Then all three came around to the front of the car. They appeared to be involved in an animated discussion. At one point, they all seemed to notice the Dodge van, and slowly moved in its direction.

At the sight, Fred felt his neck muscles constricting.

Leaving Frizzy behind, the big visitor proceeded to where Fred was perched, and gestured at him to roll down his window. Close up, the man appeared even larger, with his hair loosely tied at the back, and sideburns that made him look like a pirate. Through the sleeveless jacket appeared a two-inch lion, tattooed on his right shoulder. Fred carefully cracked his left window open.

"Hiya, bro'. Say, what a bummer," the guy said. "Like, we just blew a front tire, dig? I was just wondering, do you have a tire-wrench I could borrow?"

Through the rear-view mirror, Fred saw Shorty laboriously straining to reach the back window, and pass the contents of the van under the scrutiny of a large flash-light.

"Hey," he exclaimed, "what is your buddy doing out there?"

"Oh, pay him no mind, man. He's just trying to locate a tire-wrench. Do you have one I could borrow?"

"No, I don't."

He hoped that Leo did not detect the fear in his voice. Leo's ugly smirk seemed like a permanent fixture on his face, and made it hard to guess, whether or not he believed him.

But the man insisted: "Aren't you gonna check your tool-box?"

"There's no need. I just checked the equipment back at the garage, and noticed that the mechanic forgot to return the tire-tool I loaned him last week."

"Tough luck. Have you already called for help?"

"Yes, it should be coming at any moment."

"Well, I've gotta boogie right now. See ya."

"Right."

Both men returned to the Chevy, and started a lively discussion with Frizzy. From the van, Fred placed a hurried call to Tawny.

"The guards are not back yet," she answered. "I am still working the problem, Fred." As she hung up, he noticed that a lot of the brashness was gone from her voice.

"Uh-oh," he said. "Could it be that Tawny is starting to feel responsible for sending out valuable merchandise without any protection? Bet that in her eye, I am not very trustworthy either. What if I took the loot and disappeared?"

He was interrupted by a call from Bud. Out there, traffic was fierce.

"For godssakes, Bud, please hurry up. Things getting spooky around here."

The comm battery was down to its last drops of juice. The three men emerged from the Chevy, and slowly proceeded in his direction. Fred felt the stress in his neck muscles as he whispered: "Outnumbered three to one."

Nervously, he tugged at the tire-wrench under his seat. Three faces with the same ugly smirk got nearer. In the middle, Leo was swinging a large machete. To his right walked Shorty, armed with a long iron pipe; to his left, marched Frizzy carrying an aluminum baseball bat.

On the highway, the wild motor traffic was still rushing by.

"What if I just stepped into the midst of these cars and gestured for help?" Fred deliberated. "My chances of being killed are even greater in traffic than in a confrontation with these criminals."

On a one-by-three-feet piece of cardboard, he hastily scribbled "H-E-L-P" in large letters, turned the van's emergency lights on, and gestured with the message out of the open window. The traffic still ambled blindly by. The ambient light was too low for most motorists to see his message, and no one stopped.

As they got nearer, the faces of the three thugs seemed to exhibit a strange and almost sexual satisfaction. He heard a big pop. Shorty forcefully attacked the rear-door handle which yielded under the pressure. Coming from the right side of the van were Leo and Frizzy, unseen from the road traffic. Frizzy used his metal baseball bat to shatter the window. The smashed pane still managed to hold on for a while, even though a shower of glass shards scattered everywhere. Another thud, and the bat made a six-inch opening in the window, through which Leo's hand worked the handle, and opened the door. It all took but a few seconds.

Fred was still in the driver's seat, not moving. Leo entered the van, and emphatically deposited his machete on the passenger's seat. His face still bearing a smirk, he extended his right hand, saying: "Peace, brother?"

Instinctively, Fred gave him his hand, and Leo grabbed on to it. The next few seconds, Fred felt a powerful jab connecting with his right cheek-bone, and illuminating his vision with a shower of stars. This was followed by the sharp pain of an elbow impacting his rib cage, and forcing his body to lean forward. A powerful upper-cut met his head midway, and sent it reeling backward. The last he remembered was the powerful thud, and the wet throbbing pain in the back of his skull as it hit the driver's window. Then Leo's distorted far away voice said: "This'll keep you at peace for a while . . . for a while . . ."

The deep pulsating pain awakened him. He felt a salty wetness, and the taste of blood. He was still seated at the same place in the van.

He heard an excited voice shouting from the back of the van: "Hey guys! Get a load of this: I recognize the large letter M on these boxes of HyPelvent. A guy around the corner from me sells them for two bucks apiece! I tell you guys, this stuff is illegal! It's hot!"

The door next to him had come ajar during the fight, so he exited the van, carrying the tire-wrench and the blanket. In spite of the pain, he slowly managed to reach the front of the vehicle, proceed to the right side of the road, and disappear into the tall grass. There, he almost passed out again. The cold wind pinched him back to reality. A decision had to be made.

He returned to the road and slowly reached the back of the Chevy. From this position, he could observe his van. The back door was broken ajar. The visitors seemed to be in some hurry to retrieve the loot out of the immobilized vehicle.

He pulled on the rear license plate of the Chevy, uncovered the gas cap, and unscrewed it. In the dark, he felt the throat of the gas tank, as well as the little metal obstruction required by law to keep gasoline fumes inside. The flat end of his wrench quickly popped the small piece of metal.

He tore a long one-inch wide strip off the cotton blanket. Using the wrench, he worked it as deep as he could into the gas tank. A small length of the cloth was left hanging out of the opening. He tore another piece of the blanket, and attached it to the first one. In less than two minutes, he had tied enough lengths end-to-end to reach the cement edge of the bridge.

The first to approach was Shorty, laden with part of the cardboard boxes. Behind, the other two were busy loading up the rest. Fred hid on a small ledge behind the concrete wall. A strong odor of gasoline told him that the rudimentary wick was soaked and ready. His red and chrome lighter was in his hand. Very carefully, he gave it a flick, and lit the long jerry-rigged wick. A quick flame snaked its way to the back of the passenger car, just as he managed to hurl his aching body over the ledge. First, he felt the frigid night air rushing past his ears. Next, the landscape above him was illuminated by a powerful flash, accompanied by a booming explosion, and a rising fireball, all coming from the Chevy that had become a giant Molotov cocktail. His body entered the water of the Archer Daniel with a big splash, and the cold current took his breath away, as he sank beneath the gurgling surface.

It took a few minutes for him to come to the surface. On the bridge, the burning remains of the Chevy were going up in a large cloud of smoke. A police helicopter swept the scene with its powerful searchlight, while in the distance, police cruisers rushed in, their blue lights blinking.

THE END